AF751737

PIDGE'S POPPIES

Jan Andrews Timothy Ide

Pidge was a thoughtful little pigeon,
loyal, trustworthy and smart.
At least that's what Henry thought.

Pidge and Henry were best friends.

They loved playing I Spy.

One day, Pidge spied an enormous building.
'What's that?' she said.
'Dad calls it the War Memorial,' said Henry.
'It's where people remember those who died in wars.'

'Do they only remember people, or other animals too?' Pidge asked.

Pidge remembered stories about her many-times great-grandmother.
She had gone to the Second World War in 1939.

Then she remembered stories about her even-more-times great-grandfather who had gone to the First World War in 1914.

Thousands of pigeons were sent from Australia to the wars.

They were called carrier pigeons.

But, really, they were soldier pigeons.

Pigeons can always find their way home.

So they could carry messages from anywhere on the battlefield to their home.

Messages were written on tiny pieces of paper
and carried in little tubes.

The pigeons' home was called a pigeon loft.
It was moved around the battlefield
on the back of a small truck, like a pigeon caravan.

If the telegraph lines from the battlefront were bombed, the pigeons could still carry messages from soldiers back to headquarters. They saved many soldiers' lives.

Pidge's many-times great-grandmother
was awarded the Dickin medal!
It's for birds and other animals.
She showed 'Conspicuous gallantry or devotion
to duty while serving in military conflict'.

But the bombs and flying bullets made for dangerous work.
Sadly, many pigeons did not come back.

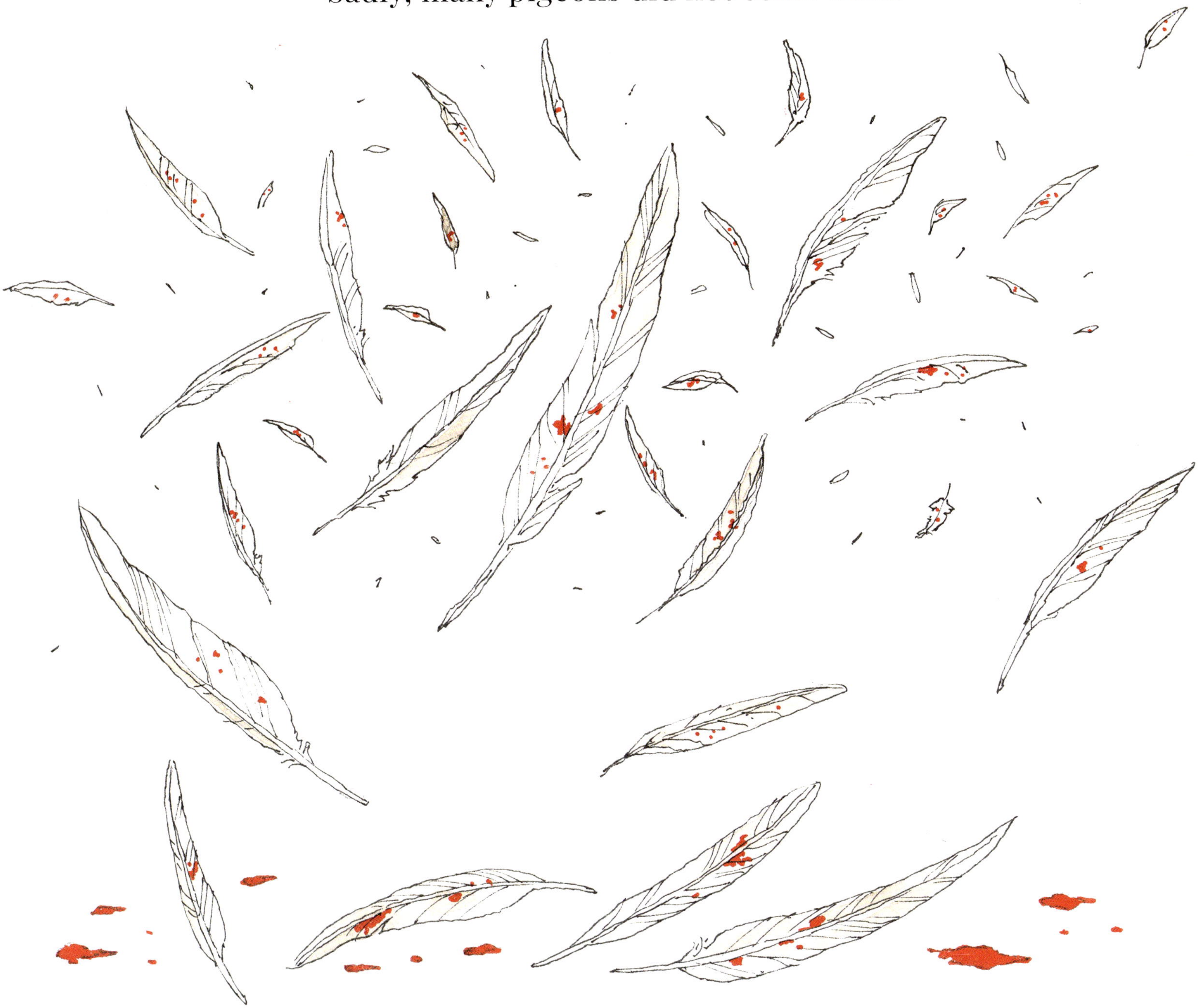

Pidge's many more times great-grandfather did not come home.

‘Let’s explore the War Memorial,’ Pidge said.

‘That’s a great idea!’ said Henry.

They flew over a long pool, past walls of bronze
covered with names and on towards some coloured glass.
'Look at all those red flowers,' said Pidge.

Pidge and Henry perched on a high ledge and
listened to one of the guides.
'Notice the tomb of the Unknown Soldier,'
the guide said,
'just below those beautiful stained-glass windows . . .
oh, look, two pigeons!'

‘Pigeons played an important role during wartime,’ she added. Pidge and Henry fluffed their feathers with pride as the guide described those brave birds.

'In the First World War, blood-red poppies bloomed
on the battlefields of Belgium and France,' the guide continued.
'So poppies became a symbol of all those who didn't return.'

‘After the war, people wore cloth poppies to remember the soldiers, particularly on Remembrance Day. They still do.

‘Visitors leave poppies beside the names of people they know, to show these soldiers are remembered.’

Just before springtime, Pidge and Henry
both felt like nesting.
'Let's build our nest at the War Memorial,' said Henry.
'That's a great idea!' said Pidge.
'And I know what we can use to build it.'

After the visitors left each day,
Pidge and Henry carefully collected
poppies to line their nest.

Guides and visitors noticed, and smiled.
And the guides explained what brave pigeons had done
in times of war.

By spring the nest was finished. It was simply beautiful.

High up, a blaze of deep red glowed in the light of the stained-glass windows. Pidge and Henry were proud of their nest.

Journalists wrote stories about the nest and what pigeons did during wartime, with pictures of Pidge and Henry.

Soon, three baby pigeons hatched,
snug in their nest of poppies . . .

for remembrance.

To Julie Slater, Mariann McNamara, Kristin Headlam and Anne Edwards – so many thanks for your support for Pidge – JA

For all the heroic animals – TI

First published by Ford Street Publishing, Melbourne, Victoria, Australia

2 4 6 8 10 9 7 5 3 1

This publication is copyright. Apart from any use as permitted under the Copyright Act 1968, no part may be reproduced by any process without prior written permission from the publisher. Requests and enquiries concerning reproduction should be addressed to Ford Street Publishing Pty Ltd, 162 Hoddle Street, Abbotsford, Vic 3067, Australia

Text copyright © Jan Andrews 2024
Illustrations copyright © Timothy Ide 2024
Illustrations produced using pen & wash

ISBN 978-1-922696-38-0 (HB)
ISBN 978-1-922696-39-7 (PB)

www.fordstreetpublishing.com
First published 2024

A catalogue record for this book is available from the National Library of Australia

Editing: Nan McNab
Design & layout: Joanne Marchese
Printed in China by Tingleman Pty Ltd